Disney's
My Very First Winnie the Pooh™
1,2,3 with Pooh

Written by
Cassandra Case

Illustrated by
Lori Tyminski and Atelier Philippe Harchy

SCHOLASTIC INC.

New York Toronto London Auckland Sydney
Mexico City New Delhi Hong Kong Buenos Aires

Published by Scholastic Inc., 90 Old Sherman Turnpike, Danbury, CT 06816
by arrangement with Disney Licensed Publishing.

SCHOLASTIC and associated logos are trademarks
and/or registered trademarks of Scholastic Inc.

ISBN 0-7172-8871-4

Printed in the U.S.A.

Early one bright, happy morning,
As Pooh licks clean a pot,
An idea pops into his head.
And then he thinks, "Why not?"

Pooh walks out, looking back and forth.
He really hopes to find
One of his friends that he can tell
The thought that's on his mind.

Kanga and Roo are passing by.
Pooh calls to them by name,
"Kanga! Roo! I had an idea
Just now before you came!"

"Christopher Robin learned to count.
Why don't we do the same?
We can all have a happy time
Playing a number game."

1

"Me first, me first!" cries little Roo.
"Look, everyone—up there!
ONE big pink-and-blue butterfly
Is dancing in the air!"

2

Piglet comes next to take his turn.
He squeaks out loud, "I spy
TWO of the giant-est acorns
To make a haycorn pie!"

3

Pooh thinks suddenly, "I know what!"
And runs on furry feet
To get THREE pots of honey down
So they can have a treat.

4

Rabbit works hard in his garden
Making the rows all neat.
Then he fills FOUR bags with carrots
For everyone to eat.

5

Tigger is very excited—
He's really feeling fine!
He gets FIVE stripey bouncing balls
And puts them in a line.

6

"Oh, look!" says Christopher Robin,
"Here's something new for you.
I've brought along SIX yellow kites
To sail up in the blue."

7

Gopher now gets his turn to play.
(It makes him smile a lot!)
He puts SEVEN purple flowers
In a little blue pot.

8

Owl comes hurrying down the path—
He wants to join the fun!
He brings along EIGHT storybooks
To read when day is done.

9

Eeyore is finally cheery
Just long enough to say,
"Look at the NINE balloons I've brought.
Don't let them get away!"

10

Now they all gather together
After their counting play—
TEN happy friends to celebrate
A Hundred-Acre day!